To ______________________

Love ______________________

First Candlewick Press hardcover edition 2003
First published in Great Britain in 1989 by Walker Books Ltd., London.

The Library of Congress has cataloged the paperback edition as follows:

Butterworth, Nick.
My dad is awesome / Nick Butterworth. — 1st U.S. ed.
Summary: A young boy extols the virtues of his father.
ISBN 1-56402-033-9 (paperback)
[1. Fathers and sons — Fiction.] I. Title.
PZ7.B98225My 1992
[E]—dc20 91-27843
ISBN 0-7636-2056-4 (hardcover)

2 4 6 8 10 9 7 5 3

Printed in Hong Kong

This book was typeset in New Century Schoolbook.
The illustrations were done in watercolor.

Candlewick Press
2067 Massachusetts Avenue
Cambridge, Massachusetts 02140

visit us at www.candlewick.com

MY DAD IS AWESOME

Nick Butterworth

CANDLEWICK PRESS
CAMBRIDGE, MASSACHUSETTS

My dad is awesome.

He’s as strong as a gorilla . . .

and he can run like a cheetah . . .

and he can play any instrument . . .

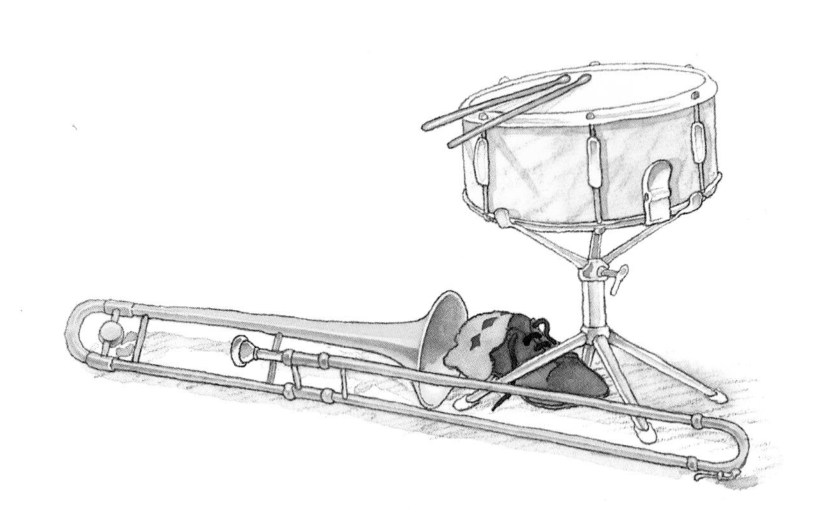

and he's a great cook . . .

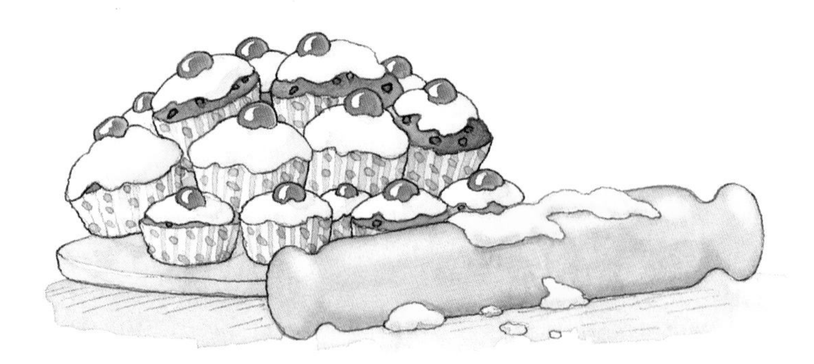

and he's fantastic
on roller skates . . .

WOW

and he's terrific at
making things . . .

and he can sing like a rock star . . .

and he can juggle anything . . .

and he's not at all
scared of the dark . . .

and he tells the funniest
jokes in the world.

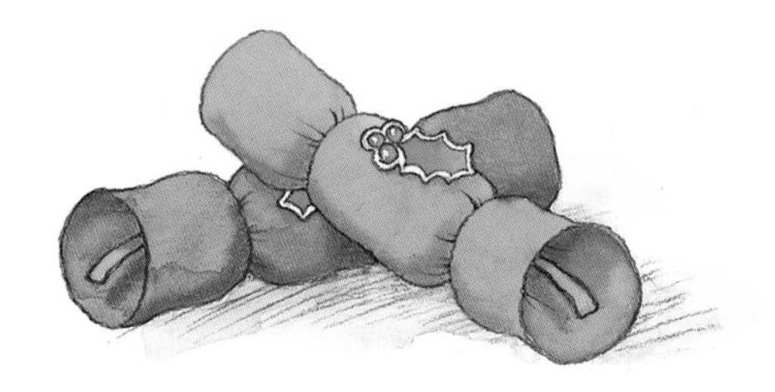

It's great to have
a dad like mine.

He's awesome!